P9-DYD-748

E
DAY

Day, Alexandra.

Carl's birthday.

$12.95

DATE			

BAKER & TAYLOR

You are invited to

Carl's

Birthday Party

on Saturday afternoon

at 4 o'clock

P.S. This is to be a
Surprise Party

CARL'S BIRTHDAY

ALEXANDRA DAY

Farrar Straus Giroux

New York

Also by Alexandra Day
Carl Goes Shopping
Carl's Christmas
Carl's Afternoon in the Park
Carl's Masquerade
Carl Goes to Daycare
Carl Makes a Scrapbook

My thanks to Sophia Moran Schafer and her parents
for their patience and cheerful cooperation.

Copyright © 1995 by Alexandra Day
All rights reserved
Library of Congress catalog card number: 94-61974
Published simultaneously in Canada by HarperCollinsCanadaLtd
Color separations by Photolitho AC
Printed and bound in the United States by Berryville Graphics
First edition, 1995

The Carl character originally appeared in *Good Dog, Carl*
by Alexandra Day, published by Green Tiger Press

"May Carl and Madeleine take their nap at your house this afternoon? I have to prepare for the P-A-R-T-Y."

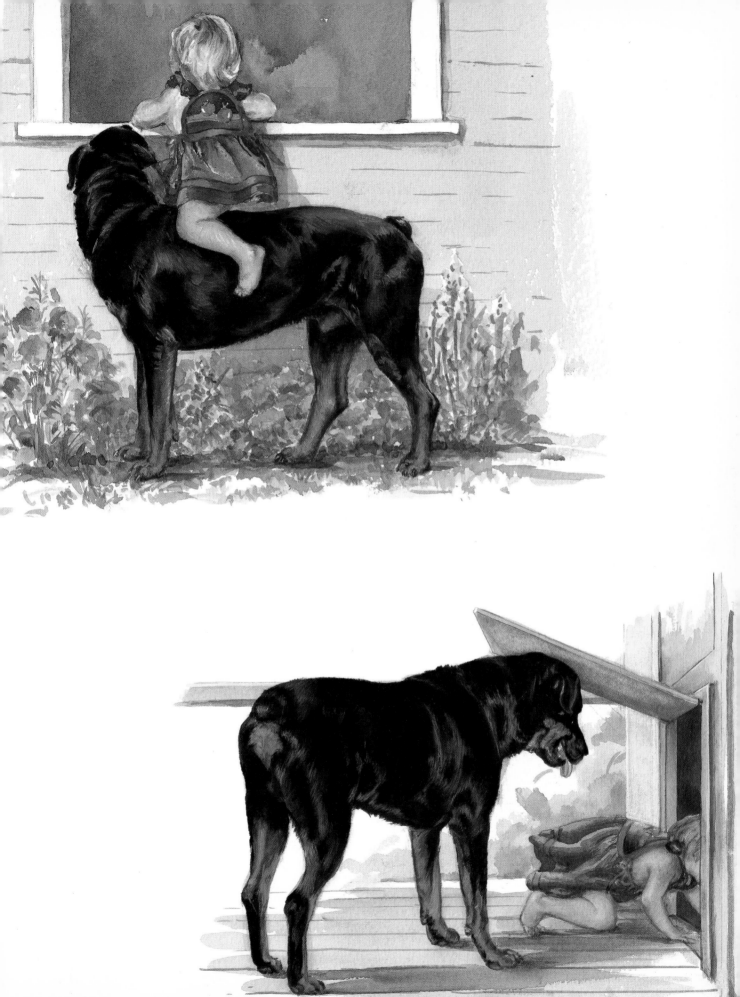

Match the Tails
Game

DRI-DOG
RAIN
PONCHO
size: Large

"Happy birthday,

Carl!"

"I hope you had a wonderful birthday, Carl. I guess we really fooled you this time."